03/16

Dear Parent:
Your child's love of reading starts here!

Every child learns to read in a different way and at his or her own speed. Some go back and forth between reading levels and read favorite books again and again. Others read through each level in order. You can help your young reader improve and become more confident by encouraging his or her own interests and abilities. From books your child reads with you to the first books he or she reads alone, there are I Can Read Books for every stage of reading:

SHARED READING
Basic language, word repetition, and whimsical illustrations, ideal for sharing with your emergent reader

BEGINNING READING
Short sentences, familiar words, and simple concepts for children eager to read on their own

READING WITH HELP
Engaging stories, longer sentences, and language play for developing readers

READING ALONE
Complex plots, challenging vocabulary, and high-interest topics for the independent reader

I Can Read Books have introduced children to the joy of reading since 1957. Featuring award-winning authors and illustrators and a fabulous cast of beloved characters, I Can Read Books set the standard for beginning readers.

A lifetime of discovery begins with the magical words "I Can Read!"

Visit www.icanread.com for information
on enriching your child's reading experience.

Visit www.zonderkidz.com for more Zonderkidz I Can Read! titles.

"Let your light shine before men, that they may
see your good deeds and praise your Father in heaven."
—*Matthew 5:16*

ZONDERKIDZ

The Berenstain Bears® Very Beary Stories
Copyright © 2018-2019 by Berenstain Publishing, Inc.
Illustrations © 2018-2019 by Berenstain Publishing, Inc.

An **I Can Read Book**

Requests for information should be addressed to:
Zonderkidz, 3900 *Sparks Dr, Grand Rapids, Michigan 49546*

ISBN 978-0-310-76842-5

The Berenstain Bears® Play a Fair Game ISBN 9780310760245
The Berenstain Bears® Respect Each Other ISBN 9780310760092
The Berenstain Bears® Get the Job Done ISBN 9780310760153

Design layout: Diane Mielke

Printed in China

20 21 22 23 24 25 LEO 10 9 8 7 6 5 4 3 2 1

ZONDERkidz™

BEGINNING
1
READING

I Can Read!

The Berenstain Bears.
Play a
Fair Game

**by Stan & Jan Berenstain
with Mike Berenstain**

Living Lights™
A Faith Story

Z | ZONDERkidz

Brother and Sister Bear

loved all kinds of sports.

In the fall, they played soccer.

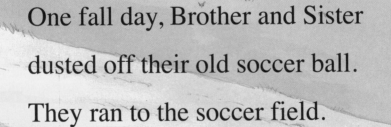

One fall day, Brother and Sister
dusted off their old soccer ball.
They ran to the soccer field.

Their team was called the Rockets.

They weren't the best,

but they were pretty good.

Papa Bear was their coach.

Their best players were

the Bruno twins, Bram and Bam.

Brother and Sister were good too.

Brother was best at corner kicks.

Sister could bop Brother's kicks

into the net with her head.

They didn't always win.

But it was fun just to play.

"Remember, team," Papa said.

"It's not if you win or lose.

It's how you play the game!"

There was one team
that only cared about winning.
They were called the Steamrollers.

Their coach said,

"It isn't how you play the game,

but if you win or lose!"

The Rockets' first game of the year
was with the Steamrollers.
"Do your best,"
Coach Papa told his team.

Mama and Honey sat in the stands.

Grizzly Gramps and Gran were there too.

Even their Sunday school teacher

Missus Ursula was there.

The Steamrollers looked huge!

So did Too-Tall Grizzly.

He was their best player.

Brother looked at Sister.

The Rockets were worried.

The referee started the game.

The Rockets had the ball.

They brought it down the field.

They passed the ball back and forth.

Bram headed for the goal.

"Take him out!" yelled
the Steamrollers' coach.
Too-Tall slide-tackled Bram.

"Foul!" yelled Coach Papa.

But the referee said,

"He was going for the ball.

No foul."

The Steamrollers scored a goal.

"How do you like that, shorty?"

Too-Tall said to Bram.

"That's enough!" said the referee.

"That is poor sportsmanship!"

said Coach Papa.

But the Steamrollers played rough.

At halftime, the score was

Steamrollers five; Rockets zero.

"You're playing a good,
clean game," said Papa.
"The Steamrollers don't play fair.
You don't want to win that way."

"It would be nice to score

a goal," said Bram.

"I know how!" said Brother.

"Let's set up a corner kick."

Brother put the ball in the corner.

He kicked hard.

Sister jumped up.

She knocked the ball into the goal.

But when Sister came down,

Too-Tall hit her hard.

"Are you okay?" asked Brother.

"I think so," said Sister.

The referee gave Too-Tall a red card.

He was out of the game.

The Steamrollers' coach

yelled at the referee.

Then Papa ran onto the field.

He started yelling too.

Soon everyone was upset.

Then Missus Ursula walked

onto the field.

"I'm very disappointed," she said.

"Is this how I taught you

to behave in Sunday school?"

"Remember," Missus Ursula said.

"Blessed are the peacemakers,

They will be called sons of God."

The coaches shook hands.

Everyone took their seats.

The game went on.

The teams played fair and had fun.

After the game, they all
had dinner at Burger Bear.
And they all felt like winners.

"Honor your father and your mother ..."
—Exodus 20:12

BEGINNING
1
READING

I Can Read!

The Berenstain Bears
Respect
Each Other

written by
Stan & Jan Berenstain
with Mike Berenstain

Living Lights™
A Faith Story

ZONDERkidz

It was a beautiful summer day.

The Bear family was going on a picnic.

Mama and Papa packed the picnic.

Brother, Sister, and Honey were ready!

Gramps and Gran were coming too.

"I made my special stew," said Gran.

"Mmm!" said Gramps. "My favorite!"

"Yuck-o!" said Brother.

Sister laughed.

"What did you say?" said Mama.

"Nothing!" said Brother.

"Come on, Sis.

Let's find a good picnic spot."

The Bear family walked
down the sunny dirt road.
Brother and Sister soon ran ahead.
They wanted to find a perfect spot
for the picnic.

"Wait for us please, cubs," said Mama.
Brother and Sister didn't listen.
Mama was not pleased.

"There's a good picnic spot
right in these trees," said Papa.
"We used to come here
when I was in school."

"That was a long time ago,"

said Sister. "It looks so old, now!

Let's find a better spot."

Papa was not pleased.

"Here's a lovely spot by the pond," said Mama. "Papa and I came here on our first date."

"You and Papa on a date?"
said Brother. "Ew!
Let's find another spot."
Mama and Papa were
not pleased.

"There's a lovely view at the top of Big Bear Hill," said Gran.

But Mama said, "We don't want to climb all that way. Let's find a nicer spot."
Gran was not pleased.

The Bear family kept walking.

They were getting hungry,

hot, and tired.

"I have an idea for a picnic spot,"

said Gramps.

But Papa said, "We don't need help. We know what we're doing."

Gramps stopped short.

"Now wait a minute!" said Gramps.

"It seems to me you all aren't

showing respect to your elders."

"That's right," Gran agreed.
"The Bible says to listen to those
who are older than you. They have
wisdom to share."

"But, Gramps!" said Papa.

"No 'buts,' Sonny!" said Gramps.

"A wise son listens to his father."

"Sonny?" said Brother and Sister.

They had never thought about how

Papa was someone's son.

Brother, Sister, Mama, and Papa
knew Gramps and Gran were right.

"We're sorry!" said Brother and Sister.

"We'll show more respect from now on."

"We're sorry too!" said Mama and Papa.

"We forgive you," said Gran.

"Now come along. Gramps will pick

the perfect picnic spot."

"Yes, indeedy!" said Gramps.

"Where are we going, Gramps?"
asked Brother and Sister as Gramps
led the way.

"Never fear," said Gramps.
"Grizzly Gramps is here!"

The Bear family marched over
hills and through fields.
"Here's the perfect spot!"
said Gramps.

"But, Gramps!" said Sister.

"That's your own house."

"Haven't you ever heard of a

backyard picnic?" said Gramps.

Gramps and Papa fired up the grill.

They heated up Gran's stew.

They grilled salmon too.

"Mmm!" said Brother and Sister.

"Salmon! That's our favorite!"

They all raised cups of lemonade to show respect for Gramps and Gran.

"To Grizzly Gramps," said Papa.

"He found the perfect picnic spot."

"Whatever your hand finds to do,
do it with all your might."
—*Ecclesiastes 9:10*

The Berenstain Bears.
Get the Job Done

written by Jan and Mike Berenstain

ZONDERkidz

It was spring in Bear Country.

That meant it was time

for spring cleaning.

Mama, Papa, Brother, Sister,

and even Honey all had jobs to do.

The Bears got right to work!

Mama hung up the rugs to clean.

Papa went to fix the railing

on the front steps.

Brother, Sister, and Honey

had to clean

the playhouse in the backyard.

They all got off to a good start.

The sun was shining.

The air was fresh.

Birds were singing.

Bright flowers bloomed

in the garden.

Mama whacked at the rugs.

Huge clouds of dirt flew out of them.

Papa used his tools.

He carved a piece of wood into

the right shape for the railing.

Brother, Sister, and Honey
had brooms and brushes,
cloths and mops, buckets of water,
and soap.

First, they were going to sweep out
the playhouse.

"Uh-oh!" said Brother,

looking inside. "Spiders!"

Sister and Honey peeked inside.

There were big, hairy spiders.

"Yuck!" they all said.

"Let's not sweep out the inside,"
said Brother. "Let's scrub the outside.
Maybe that will scare the spiders."
So that's what they did.

Then Brother spotted

an old baseball, a bat,

and a glove behind the playhouse.

Brother picked up the ball.

Sister picked up the bat.

Brother tossed the ball to Sister.

She hit it.

"You be the outfielder, Honey,"
said Brother. He gave her the glove.
Honey crawled through the grass
and sat down.

Back at the tree house,

Mama and Papa were hard at work.

Mama was almost done with the rugs.

Papa was finishing the railing.

He stood up and stretched.

Papa saw Honey

sitting in the middle of the yard.

"What is Honey doing there?"

thought Papa.

A baseball landed

near Honey.

She picked it up and threw it.

"Hmmm!" said Papa.

Papa walked around the tree house.

He saw the cubs playing baseball.

Their brooms, brushes, cloths, and mops

were on the ground.

"This doesn't look like
spring cleaning!" said Papa.
Brother and Sister tried to hide
the ball and bat.

Papa looked at the dirty playhouse.

"You did not clean at all!" said Papa.

"There are spiders in there!"

said Sister.

Papa smiled. He knew how scary

spiders can be.

"I'll get the spiders out,"
said Papa. "Then you can
get the job done."

Papa chased the spiders away.

Then Brother, Sister, and Honey

got to work.

Mama came to see what was going on.

She saw the cubs hard at work.

"The Bible says to enjoy your work,"

said Mama.

"Did you enjoy your work, Mama?"

asked Brother.

"I enjoy my clean rugs," she said.

"And you will enjoy your clean playhouse."

"We will enjoy it," said Sister.

"But without those spiders!"

It was a job well done.